Your First Step

HENRI SORENSEN

Your First Step

Lothrop, Lee & Shepard Books
New York

Copyright © 1996 by Henri Sorensen

All rights reserved. No part of this book may be reproduced or utilized in any form or by any means,
electronic or mechanical, including photocopying and recording, or by any information storage and retrieval system,
without permission in writing from the Publisher. Inquiries should be addressed to
Lothrop, Lee & Shepard Books, a division of William Morrow & Company, Inc., 1350 Avenue of the Americas,
New York, New York 10019.

Printed in the United States of America

First Edition   1 2 3 4 5 6 7 8 9 10

Library of Congress Cataloging in Publication Data

Sorensen, Henri. Your first step / by Henri Sorensen.

p.   cm.   Summary: Describes the first steps of a baby, as well as the activities
of many different animals in other places around the world, all happening at the very same moment.

ISBN 0-688-14667-8. — ISBN 0-688-14668-6 (lib. bdg.)

[1. Animals—Fiction. 2. Babies—Fiction.] I. Title.

PZ7.S7185Yo 1996 [E]—dc20 95-44222 CIP AC

The illustrations in this book were done in acrylic paints. The display type was set in Fine Hand. The text was set in Fine Hand.
Separations by Colotone Graphics. Printed and bound by Worzalla Publishing Company. Production supervision by Cliff Bryant.

To Betsy and Ted Lewin

*A*ll at the same moment,
wolf pups in Canada
romped in the morning sun,

young otters slid down mud banks
in the English afternoon,

and lion cubs played
as the sun set over the Serengeti Plain.

*A*ll at the same moment,
jackrabbits in Arizona
were having their breakfast,

Chimpanzees in Sierra Leone
were quietly grooming each other
in the heat of the afternoon,

and in the darkness of night,
young Indian tigers were learning to hunt.

All at the same moment,
Atlantic dolphins were leaping in the noonday sun,

and as the day ended,

East African elephants drank at the water hole.

And all at the same moment
that wolf pups romped
and young otters slid
and lion cubs played
and jackrabbits ate breakfast
and chimpanzees groomed
and tigers hunted
and dolphins leapt
and elephants drank,
you, my precious baby,
let go of the branch you were hanging onto,
looked up at me and laughed,
and took your first steps all alone!

Because the earth spins as it
travels around the sun, the sun shines on
different parts of the world
at different times.
When the sun is setting in Kenya,
it is rising in Arizona, and when it is
high noon in Argentina, it is midnight
in Japan. Somewhere in the world,
somebody is getting up, somebody is
eating lunch, and somebody else is going
to bed, all at the same moment.